Fizz

4

D0269096

For Rodney, Austin
and Georgia. L.G.

For Zowie and Muttley.
S.M.K.

First published by Allen & Unwin in 2016

Allen & Unwin
83 Alexander Street
Crows Nest NSW 2065
Australia
Phone: (61 2) 8425 0100
Email: info@allenandunwin.com
Web: www.allenandunwin.com

A Cataloguing-in-Publication entry is available
from the National Library of Australia
www.trove.nla.gov.au

ISBN 978 1 76011 289 9

Cover and text design by Stephen Michael King and Trish Hayes
Set in 15pt Berkeley Oldstyle Book by Trish Hayes, Stingart
Printed in Australia by McPherson's Printing Group

10 9 8 7 6 5 4 3 2 1

MIX
Paper from
responsible sources
FSC® C001695
www.fsc.org

The paper in this book is FSC® certified.
FSC® promotes environmentally responsible,
socially beneficial and economically viable
management of the world's forests.

www.lesleygibbes.com
www.stephenmichaelking.com

FiZZ

and the
HANDBAG
DOGNAPPER

LESLEY GIBBES

ILLUSTRATED BY

STEPHEN MICHAEL KING

ALLEN&UNWIN

SYDNEY · MELBOURNE · AUCKLAND · LONDON

Remi
Razzle

Kiki

Milo

Crystal

Fizz's family

Viktor Shrill

Tom Whittaker

Cynthia

CONTENTS

With special thanks to Margaret Connolly, Sue Flockhart, Erica Wagner, Stephen Michael King and Trish Hayes.

L.G.

Fizz arrived for work at Sunnyvale City Police Station and straightaway smelled trouble. He'd never seen Sergeant Stern look so worried before.

'I'd like to speak to you in my office,' said the sergeant. Remi and Amadeus were already sitting by the desk.

'What's happening?' whispered Fizz.

'It's a special undercover assignment,' said Remi, swishing her tail excitedly. 'Sergeant Stern called me in this morning. I think it has something to do with the Handbag Dognapper.'

Fizz shivered.

Sergeant Stern and the team at Sunnyvale City Police Station had been working on the case of the Handbag Dognapper all week. Two handbag dogs had been kidnapped from red-carpet events in Sunnyvale City, and no one knew who was doing it or why. They hadn't even received a ransom note!

Sergeant Stern opened the police file on his desk and pulled out two photographs: a miniature tan Pug, and a white Chihuahua. Fizz recognised the dogs immediately. Milo and Kiki. Milo was the model for Pierre Le Trende's manbag range. Kiki went everywhere with the singer Sassy Starlet.

'I'm afraid I have bad news,' said
Sergeant Stern, pulling a third photograph
from his file. 'The Handbag Dognapper has
struck again!'

Fizz's skin prickled with anticipation.
Who would the next handbag victim be?

'I'm sorry, Fizz,' said Sergeant Stern,
holding up a photograph of a white
Bolognese. 'The Handbag Dognapper's latest
victim is Crystal.'

Fizz yelped. Crystal was his sister. She
was the handbag dog for a famous actress

who always took her to special events. Fizz's family had been worried for Crystal's safety ever since the first kidnapping.

'I'm so sorry, Fizz,' said Remi, giving him a comforting nuzzle.

'Bad news,' said Amadeus.

Fizz shook his head. *Not Crystal!*

'W-what happened?' he asked.

'Crystal went missing from the movie premiere of *Puppy Tales II* last night,' said Sergeant Stern. 'Her celebrity companion left her at the buffet table while she signed autographs. When she returned, Crystal was gone.

'All we found was a half-eaten slice of bacon cake with white liver sprinkles.'

'I've never heard of white liver sprinkles,' said Amadeus, shaking his head.

'Neither have I,' said Sergeant Stern. 'I've sent the cake to the lab for testing, but the results won't be back until tomorrow.'

'Tomorrow!' said Fizz. 'There must be something we can do *today*!'

'There is,' said Sergeant Stern. 'You, Remi and Amadeus are going undercover immediately!'

Chapter 2

The Bait

Sergeant Stern swung on his backpack, and Fizz, Remi and Amadeus followed him through the glass doors of Sunnyvale City Police Station and down busy Main Street.

They passed the poodle parlour and the butcher shop. 'Where are we going Sergeant Stern?' asked Fizz.

'I'm sending the three of you undercover at today's big red-carpet event in the city,' said Sergeant Stern, crossing the road and stopping on the pavement outside Sunnyvale City Park.

'At the park?' asked Amadeus.

Sergeant Stern nodded.

'The Shrill Alarm Collar launch is being held in the Grand Gazebo here at Sunnyvale City Park today,' he said, taking the backpack off his shoulder. 'The launch is attracting celebrities from all over the country.'

'What's an alarm collar?'
asked Fizz.

'The Shrill Alarm Collar is
a personal safety alarm for dogs,
invented by a businessman named
Viktor Shrill. The collar has an
inbuilt siren, with flashing lights,
to scare away any would-be attacker.
I believe the Handbag Dognapper
will strike at the launch today, and
when he does I want you, Fizz, to
be his next victim.'

Fizz trembled. Being snatched by the Handbag Dognapper was sure to be dangerous.

'Are we going to be celebrity guests at the launch?' asked Remi, bouncing on her tippy toes.

'No,' said Sergeant Stern, 'you won't be watching the launch, Remi, you'll be part of it. The three of you have been hired to model the Shrill Alarm Collar on the catwalk today.'

'We're going undercover as *models*,' said Amadeus, his jaw dropping. 'I won't have to wear a costume, will I, Sergeant Stern?'

'Yes, you will. But only Fizz will be in a handbag. He'll be our bait for the Handbag Dognapper.'

'You were born for this, Powder Puff,' said Amadeus.

'How can I catch the Handbag Dognapper if *he* kidnaps *me*?' said Fizz.

'You won't be catching him,' said Sergeant Stern. 'I will. The plan is for you to lead me to his hideout with this.'

Sergeant Stern pulled a collar and receiver box out of his bag.

'It's a tracker,' said Sergeant Stern. 'If you're kidnapped, I'll be able to track your movements to the Handbag Dognapper's hideout and make the arrest.'

Fizz sat still as Sergeant Stern buckled the tracker collar around his neck.

'Keep the tracker hidden at all times and never take it off. If you lose it, I won't know where you are and you'll have to handle the Handbag Dognapper on your own!'

Sergeant Stern pressed a red activation button on the collar. A map of Sunnyvale City Park flashed on the receiver screen, with a red dot showing Fizz's location.

Fizz shook his fur over the tracker to hide it.

'Remi and Amadeus, your job is to keep an eye on Fizz, and to make sure everything runs smoothly. Alert me the second Fizz goes missing. I'll need you both to assist me during the rescue and arrest.'

Remi and Amadeus both wagged.

Sergeant Stern checked his watch.

'Cynthia Sharp, the events coordinator, is expecting three dogs from the Stern Modelling agency at 10 a.m. It's time to go!' he said. 'Stay alert, and remember I'll be just outside the park watching.'

Fizz took a deep breath.

Chapter 3
The Handbag

izz didn't want to waste a moment. He ran with Remi and Amadeus through the bougainvillea archway to the centre of Sunnyvale City Park.

'Wow!' said Fizz, looking at the Grand Gazebo.

The Shrill Alarm Collar launch was a spectacular event. Stylish white tables covered the lawns and the gazebo was decorated with flags. There was a big banner that read: The Shrill Alarm Collar. Because We Care.

Fizz's heart raced as he walked the red carpet with Remi and Amadeus to the entry.

'Wonderful, you're here!' said a woman with a clipboard. She had a nametag that said: Cynthia Sharp, Event Coordinator.

Cynthia flipped through the papers on her clipboard.

'I have your portfolio photographs,' she said, looking at Fizz, Remi and Amadeus. 'But I seem to be missing your names.'

Fizz almost panicked. He'd forgotten all about an undercover name. His last undercover name, Angel, made him sound like a girl. This time, he was determined to choose something fiercer.

'My name's Brock,' said
Amadeus, flexing his
muscles.

'And I'm Veronica,' said Remi,
leaping into a scissor split.

'And your name is…?' asked Cynthia,
waiting for an answer.

'My name's…Poncho,' blurted Fizz.

'Cute,' said Cynthia, bending down and
fluffing the fur on Fizz's head.

Amadeus muffled a laugh.

Fizz couldn't believe what he'd just said.
Poncho! He shook out the frizz from his fur.

'Right,' said Cynthia, pointing across the lawn. 'Your stylist is Tarquin, and he has your costumes ready. Wardrobe is located backstage, behind the Grand Gazebo. It's the green tent with the fringed flap. The yellow marquee with the Shrill logo above the door is for Viktor Shrill. It's strictly out of bounds.'

'What does the logo look like?' asked Fizz.

'It's a little bird called the Golden-throated Honeyeater,' said Cynthia. 'It's so rare that it's found only on the grounds of Viktor Shrill's estate in Blue Haven. Viktor modelled the collar's alarm on the bird's shrieking call.'

'It must be very loud,' said Remi, flattening her ears.

'It's ear-splitting!' said Cynthia. 'Wait till we demonstrate the collar at the launch.'

Cynthia waved them away.

'I'll collect you from your dressing rooms when it's time for the show,' she said. 'And remember, no wandering about the park. I want your costumes in pristine condition for the catwalk.'

'Costumes?' whined Amadeus. 'Mine better show off my physique!'

The dogs made their way past the Grand Gazebo to the wardrobe tent.

'Fringed flap. I think this is it,' said Fizz.

Inside were racks of dazzling costumes, hats and glitzy accessories. A slim man wearing a fancy vest and crimson pants met them with open arms.

'Welcome! My name is Tarquin,' he gushed, 'and I'm your stylist today. Please take a dressing podium.'

He herded them across the marquee to three mint-green dressing boxes beside a costume rack.

'Up you get. Up! Up! Up!' he said, clapping his hands.

Fizz, Remi and Amadeus jumped onto a box and waited.

'Relax, Powder Puff,' said Amadeus. 'All you have to do is fit in that handbag. Remi and I will be making the arrest with Sergeant Stern when you get kidnapped.'

Fizz took a calming breath.

'I have a really fun look for each of you today,' said Tarquin, taking two costumes from the rack. He put a glow-in-the-dark headband on Remi's head and a matching anklet on each paw. Then he placed a pair of dark sunglasses over Amadeus's eyes and a bandanna around his neck.

'Cool,' said Amadeus, checking himself out in the mirror.

Tarquin smiled at Fizz. 'And I have a super-fun handbag for you!' He took a dazzling gold-feathered handbag from the costume rack. '*Voilà!*'

Fizz's eyes popped. The handbag was tiny! He put his front paws into the bag. He wriggled and squeezed and worked his back legs in, but no matter how he positioned himself, he was sticking out.

'Oh dear!' said Tarquin. 'You are rather plus size for a handbag dog!'

Fizz looked up at Tarquin. If he was going to be kidnapped by the Handbag Dognapper, he *had* to fit in a handbag.

'I'll have to find you another costume,' said Tarquin, rummaging through the racks.

Fizz didn't want another costume, he wanted a handbag. Suddenly he had an idea.

'Manbag!' barked Fizz. 'I'll fit in a manbag. They're the latest in handbag fashion for men.'

Tarquin's face brightened.

'You're right,' he said. 'Manbags are definitely in!'

He disappeared behind a stack of hats and boxes, then returned with a striped gym bag.

'Let's try this,' he said, scooping Fizz's fringe behind a sweatband and opening the gym bag.

Fizz jumped in.

The manbag was much roomier.

'Cute look, Powder Puff,' said Amadeus.

Fizz didn't care. He was in a handbag and wearing his tracker collar. All he needed now was the Handbag Dognapper.

Chapter 4

The Collar

arquin clapped his hands. 'Into line everyone, Viktor's here!'

Fizz sat in his manbag next to Remi and Amadeus. Standing at the entry was a man in a striped suit with a neat goatee beard. Viktor Shrill! And he was holding three Shrill Alarm Collars.

'Your models are in costume and ready for the launch, Mr Shrill,' said Tarquin. 'I see you've brought the alarm collars.'

Viktor nodded.

Fizz studied the collars. They were yellow and green with a silver activation button.

Viktor strode across the marquee to Amadeus and buckled a Shrill Alarm Collar around his neck. Fizz fidgeted in his manbag as Viktor spoke.

'The Shrill Alarm Collar – why?' said Viktor, buckling a collar around Remi's neck. 'Because I care. I truly do. It breaks my heart to think about those three poor little dogs whisked away by the Handbag Dognapper. If only someone had been there to protect them. That's why I invented the Shrill Alarm Collar.'

Fizz gulped. Now all he could think about was Crystal and how scared and alone she must feel, locked up by the Handbag Dognapper. Fizz was so worried for Crystal that he barely felt Viktor unbuckle his tracker collar and replace it with the Shrill Alarm. By the time he saw Viktor slip the tracker into his coat pocket and leave, it was too late.

'What's wrong?' asked Remi.

'The tracker,' gasped Fizz. 'It's gone!'

Chapter 5

The Bacon Cake

Remi and Amadeus slumped on the cushions in their dressing-room marquee.

'We've got to get the tracker back from Viktor before the launch starts,' said Fizz, jumping out of the gym bag, 'or Sergeant Stern won't be able to follow me to the kidnapper's hideout.'

'But how?' said Remi, raising her eyebrows. 'We're not allowed out of our dressing room until the launch, and Viktor's marquee is strictly out of bounds. If Cynthia sees us, she'll go ballistic.'

Fizz paced the floor. 'What we need is someone to keep Cynthia occupied while we sneak into Viktor's marquee to the get the tracker back.'

'I'll go,' said Amadeus, standing up straight. 'What do you want me to do?'

'An urgent wardrobe malfunction should do the trick,' said Fizz, biting a hole in Amadeus's bandanna. 'That should keep Cynthia busy.'

'I'm on it!' said Amadeus, bounding out of the marquee to find Cynthia.

'Let's go,' barked Fizz. 'We don't have much time.' Fizz and Remi snuck out the back of their dressing room.

'Viktor's marquee is the yellow one,' said Fizz, racing over and wriggling his head under the canvas.

Inside, Viktor had a laptop computer on his desk, and the walls of the tent were lined with graphs and pie charts showing sales figures and profit margins. Viktor was deep in conversation with a muscular man with a broad nose and a neck as thick as a tree trunk. Fizz and Remi stayed low.

'You know what to do, Cadmus,' said Viktor, looking at the charts.

Cadmus nodded.

'Three more ought to do the trick,' said Viktor. 'And a big one, too, for broad market appeal.'

Viktor handed Cadmus a vial of white powder and a plate of food.

'Use plenty this time,' he said. 'You want them out cold. Go to their dressing room now and make sure you're not seen.'

Cadmus walked towards the marquee door, then stopped abruptly.

'What do you want me to do with them?' he grunted.

'You can dump them, all of them… tonight!'

Cadmus pushed open the tent flaps roughly and left. Fizz and Remi pulled their heads back from under the marquee.

'Did you hear that?' said Fizz.

'What do you think they were talking about? Three more *what* ought to do what trick?' said Remi, pricking her ears. 'And what was he going to dump?'

'I don't know, but I've got a bad feeling about this,' said Fizz. 'Whatever they're up to, it has something to do with our dressing rooms. Come on, I want to find out what's going on.'

Fizz and Remi snuck along the line of marquees and back into their dressing room.

'I can't see Cadmus anywhere and there's nothing out of place,' said Remi, flopping onto a cushion.

Fizz's chest fell. Everything was in the same place except for three slices of bacon cake placed on the floor. Fizz's stomach grumbled. He hadn't eaten since breakfast.

'Catering must have delivered the cake as a pre-launch snack,' said Remi.

Just then, Amadeus burst back into the tent. He was wearing a new bandanna and grinning from ear to ear.

'You should have seen Cynthia's face when she saw the hole in the bandanna,' said Amadeus. 'She was so mad I thought she was going to lay an egg!'

Amadeus spied the bacon cake and wolfed down a slice. Then he stumbled across the dressing room and flopped onto a cushion.

'I hope Amadeus isn't going to be that clumsy on the catwalk,' said Fizz.

'We *are* supposed to be models.'

'Five minutes until launch,' called
Cynthia from outside.

'We'd better go back and get the tracker,'
said Remi, taking a bite of bacon cake.

Fizz nodded, but he just couldn't shake
the feeling that something wasn't right. He
thought about Viktor's strange conversation
with Cadmus, and Crystal's half-eaten slice
of bacon cake with white liver sprinkles,
just like the one in front of him.

Remi gave a big yawn as Fizz took
a bite of cake.

'Does this bacon cake taste weird
to you?' asked Fizz.

Remi didn't answer.

Fizz felt dizzy and his legs began to wobble.

'Oh no,' said Fizz, as the clues fell into place. 'The Handbag Dognapper is Viktor Shrill and…*you*.'

Fizz fell to the floor, as Cadmus flipped Remi over his shoulder and scooped Amadeus into his arms.

Chapter 6

Trapped

'Fizz, it *is* you!'

Fizz opened his eyes. It was dark, but standing over him were the kidnapped dogs, Crystal, Milo and Kiki.

'We're saved,' cried Crystal, licking Fizz's fur. 'We've been so scared!'

Amadeus and Remi woke up on the ground beside Fizz.

'What happened? Where are we?' asked Amadeus, shaking his head. He looked about the darkened shed.

'We've been kidnapped by the Handbag Dognapper,' said Fizz. 'That wasn't white liver sprinkles on the bacon cake. It was sleeping powder!'

'Who was it?' asked Remi, blinking. 'I didn't see anyone!'

'It's Viktor Shrill and his henchman Cadmus. By the time I worked out they were the kidnappers it was too late. We'd already eaten the bacon cake.'

Amadeus pulled himself up, but his legs were shaky. 'Why are they kidnapping dogs?' he said.

'Don't you see?' said Fizz. 'It's all about sales. "Three more ought to do the trick." Three more kidnapped dogs will see Shrill Alarm Collar sales skyrocket. They're kidnapping dogs to make everyone buy the Shrill Alarm Collar. The more dogs are kidnapped, the more scared everyone gets, the more Shrill Alarm Collars they sell.'

'That's why there's no ransom,' said Remi. 'Viktor doesn't need one, he's getting rich on collar sales!'

'If Viktor doesn't need us for a ransom then why is he keeping us, Powder Puff?' barked Amadeus.

'He's not,' said Fizz, remembering Viktor's conversation in the marquee. 'He's going to dump us. Tonight! We have to escape *now*!'

'Isn't Sergeant Stern coming?' asked Crystal, her tail drooping.

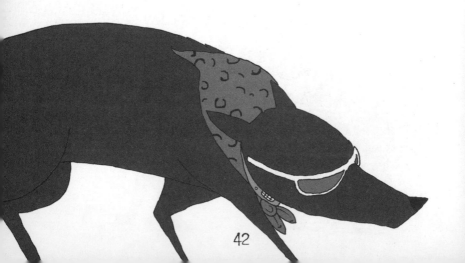

42

'Our rescue hasn't exactly gone to plan,' said Fizz, standing up and stretching his legs. 'Viktor took my tracker collar. Sergeant Stern thinks we're still at the launch. We're going to have to save ourselves.'

The only opening in the shed was a small, high window beside the locked door. Fizz scrambled up a pile of crates stacked against the wall and peered out the window.

'Can you see anything?' asked Remi, looking towards the light.

A small flutter of movement caught Fizz's eye. A bird? It had yellow feathers on its chest. When it landed on a bush, it opened its beak and gave a very loud call.

'That's a Golden-throated Honeyeater!' cried Fizz. 'The Shrill logo! I know where we are. We're on Viktor Shrill's estate in Blue Haven! Not so far from the Police Academy. If we escape, we can make our way to the Blue Haven Police Academy for Dogs and raise the alarm.'

Fizz craned his neck to see the door. It was locked from the outside with a wedge of timber. 'I could unlock the door if you can get me out.'

'We've been digging a hole,' said Crystal, 'but it's not very big. See there…'

Amadeus leapt to the hole and began to dig. His enormous paws and powerful legs sent earth flying.

Fizz's ears pricked to the sound of heavy footsteps. Boots!

'Someone's coming,' he said.

'I'm through,' said Amadeus, as a small shaft of light shone from the hole. 'Is this big enough?'

Fizz squeezed through the tunnel. He was out! He raced around and jumped to knock the timber that was holding the door. It took three tries before the timber fell.

The shed door swung open and Amadeus, Remi, Crystal, Milo and Kiki tumbled out.

Trudging towards them through the bushes was a big muscular man with a cricket bat under his arm.

'It's Cadmus!' yelled Fizz. 'Run!'

Chapter 7

The Escape

'Get back here, you mutts!' bellowed Cadmus, as he thundered down the track after Fizz and the gang. 'Run!' yelled Fizz.

The little dogs raced along a track
through a dark forest of trees, with Amadeus
behind them.

Fizz saw some light ahead.

'Follow me,' he said, as he burst out onto a manicured lawn.

'Where are we?' barked Amadeus.

'It's Viktor's estate,' said Fizz, scanning the scene.

The estate was spectacular. A topiary garden with ornate fountains and marble statues stretched towards a magnificent Spanish villa.

'We have to find a way out before Cadmus gets us,' said Fizz.

'But how?' panted Remi. 'The whole place is fenced. Maybe I could leap over?'

Fizz thought fast. 'Every fence has a gate,' he said, wagging his tail. 'We'll head towards the villa entrance.'

Suddenly Amadeus snarled. Cadmus was on the lawn behind them. Amadeus turned to face him, growling.

'No!' barked Remi. 'He'll hit you!'

'This way!' yelled Fizz,
racing through the garden.
He weaved and dodged through
bushes and statues, hoping to
shake Cadmus off their tail.
'He's still behind us,' yelled Remi,
the whites of her eyes flashing.

Cadmus was waving the bat and gaining
on them – fast. His enormous steps were

too big for Milo and Kiki. Fizz had to find
a way to slow Cadmus down.

Amadeus stopped again and looked
ready to leap, but Fizz barked, 'Head to the
trees!' He pelted full speed into an olive
grove, then skidded to a stop when he spied
a garden hose.

'Amadeus, grab the hose!' cried Fizz,
as Remi and the others dashed past. 'I've got
a plan.'

Amadeus grabbed one end of the hose
and Fizz grabbed the other.

'Lay it between the trees,' barked Fizz.
'Quick! He's coming. *Pull.*'

Fizz and Amadeus tugged the hose tight.
Cadmus tripped and fell face-first onto the
lawn.

'That should slow him down,' said Amadeus. 'Come on!'

Fizz and Amadeus caught up with Remi and the little dogs.

'We're not far from the villa,' barked Fizz. 'Keep running!'

Fizz led the gang past a glistening swimming pool and onto a gravel driveway that wound around the side of the villa.

'There's the gate,' yelled Fizz, 'and it's opening! Now's our chance to escape.'

Milo and Kiki dashed ahead.

Fizz slid to a halt. His stomach leapt. Something wasn't right.

'Milo, Kiki, stop!' he yelled.

A black shadow crept though the gate like a wolf. A limousine! Fizz gasped as the car door flew open and a man with a goatee beard stepped out. Viktor Shrill! In a flash, Viktor caught Milo and Kiki in his arms.

'I thought I told you to get rid of these mutts!' he shouted.

'Fizz, help!' cried Crystal.

Fizz spun around. Cadmus had Crystal clamped under his arm.

'Go back in the shed or the fluff ball gets it!' grunted Cadmus, squeezing Crystal hard.

Fizz's heart thumped in his chest. He had to do something. He shook the Shrill Alarm Collar around his neck, then he looked at Remi and Amadeus.

'Now!' he barked.

Fizz, Remi and Amadeus threw their chins out and activated their alarms. An ear-splitting sound shrieked across the estate and their collar lights flashed. Viktor and Cadmus recoiled in surprise. Fizz saw his chance.

'Go!' he yelled.

Fizz and Remi sprinted across the driveway to Viktor. Fizz rammed Viktor's legs and Remi jumped onto his chest. Viktor toppled to the ground, and Milo and Kiki tumbled out of his grip.

Amadeus lunged at Cadmus. He pushed
him down onto the gravel and jumped onto
his chest. When he bared his teeth, Cadmus
released his hold on Crystal.

'We got them!' yelled Fizz. He had a
grip on Viktor's wrist while Remi held fast
to his beard.

A sudden wail of police sirens filled the
air. Sergeant Stern rushed through the gate.

'How did he find us?' said Amadeus,
swatting Cadmus with his bristly tail.

'The tracker!' said Fizz, feeling a bulge in Viktor's coat. 'It's still in Viktor's coat pocket. Viktor led Sergeant Stern straight to his own hideout!'

Sergeant Stern strode across to Viktor and looked down at him.

'You won't be selling anything for a very long time,' he said, as he snapped handcuffs on Viktor and Cadmus.

59

Sergeant Stern nodded at Fizz, Remi and Amadeus. 'Great job, team. You caught the Handbag Dognappers and safely rescued the kidnapped dogs.'

'Whoo-hoo!' barked Fizz, with relief.

Chapter

The Party

'They're here!' shouted Benny, from the veranda.

Fizz, Crystal, Remi and Amadeus looked out the window of the police paddy wagon as it drove up to Sunnyvale Boarding House for Dogs.

'It's a hero's welcome!' said Sergeant Stern, parking the wagon in front of a crowd of family and friends. 'Enjoy yourselves. You've earned it! But don't stay up too late, you're all on crowd patrol in the city tomorrow morning. We're expecting big queues for the Shrill Alarm Collar.'

'What?' said Fizz.

'*Returns*, not sales,' laughed Sergeant Stern, as he headed for the buffet table.

Fizz jumped out onto the lawn with Remi, Amadeus and Crystal. His family rushed to greet them.

'Fizz! Crystal!' cried Fizz's mother. 'You're safe!'

Fizz's parents, Bella, Puff-Pup and Fluff-Pup raced over and gave Fizz, Crystal, Remi and Amadeus a happy group hug with lots of tail wagging.

'I'm so proud of you, sugarplum,' said Fizz's mother. 'You rescued our Crystal and brought her home!'

'Well done, son,' said Fizz's father. 'You're a real hero.'

Fizz was so proud he thought he might burst.

Then Tom Whittaker, the grounds-keeper, stepped up to give Fizz a firm, approving pat.

'I wasn't worried for a second,' said Tom. 'The Handbag Dognapper didn't stand a chance. Go on, off you go. It's time for you to party!'

Fizz was so excited to play with his brothers and sisters again. They were romping and chasing until they were all puffed out. Remi showed them some dance moves, and Benny boogied until his paws hurt. It was almost dark before they took a break.

'I can't believe you went undercover with Amadeus,' said Benny, flopping onto the lawn with Fizz and Remi.

'I know,' laughed Fizz. 'He still calls me Powder Puff, but we made an awesome team. Amadeus was great!'

Benny's stomach rumbled. 'Come on, let's get some food. I'm ravenous.'

Fizz, Remi and Benny made their way to the buffet table where Razor and Bruno were helping themselves to a platter of cold sausages.

'I suppose you think you're a big hero now,' growled Razor, circling Fizz.

'Yeah, a hero,' said Bruno with a mouth full of sausage.

Razor bared his teeth. 'Once a fluffy dog, always a fluffy dog,' he was saying, as Amadeus joined the group. 'So, what was it like working with this loser?'

'He's not a loser and his name is Fizz,' said Amadeus, standing by Fizz's side. He glared at Razor and Bruno. Then Amadeus gave Fizz a playful nudge.

'You can be on my team any day,' said Amadeus.

'No way!' barked Fizz. 'You can be on mine!'

Remi did a spectacular dog-flip and said, 'Well, if you want to be on *my* team, you'd better start dancing!'

'You're on!' said Amadeus.

'Right on!' barked Fizz.

Have you read all the books in the Fizz series?

From the Author and the Illustrator

When Lesley Gibbes discovered that her father-in-law's childhood nickname was 'Fizz', she knew it was the perfect name for her fluffy undercover police dog. But it was her two naughty Jack Russell terriers, Porsche and Cosworth, who were the real inspiration for Fizz. Just like Fizz, they're clever, brave and fast. And even though they are only the size of a tomcat, they both think they're as big and as bold as a German Shepherd.

When Stephen Michael King was a boy he liked to draw dogs: dogs scuba diving, driving cars, playing guitar or flying into outerspace… anything he could imagine a normal dog doing on any normal day. Now Stephen is married with two grown children, one parrot and three dogs, and he still finds himself drawing dogs: dogs in cars, on motorbikes, dressed in silly costumes and chasing robbers.

Their picture book *Scary Night*, written by Lesley Gibbes and illustrated by Stephen Michael King, was named an Honour Book in the 2015 CBCA Book of the Year Awards for Early Childhood.